D1454927

ISBN 978-1-84135-787-4

Adapted by Jane Carruth
Illustrated by Rene Cloke

Copyright © 2010 Award Publications Limited

All rights reserved. No part of this publication may be reproduced or
utilized in any form or by any means electronic or mechanical, including
photocopying, recording, or by any information storage and retrieval
system now known or hereafter invented, without the prior
written permission of the publisher.

This edition first published 2010

Published by Award Publications Limited,
The Old Riding School, The Welbeck Estate,
Worksop, Nottinghamshire, S80 3LR

10 1

Printed in China

The Wind in the Willows

Mr Toad
Comes Home

From Kenneth Grahame's
Classic Stories

Award Publications Limited

Toad was full of his adventures when at last he reached Ratty's house.

"You had better sit down," Ratty said, "and tell me why you are dressed in that ridiculous outfit."

Toad was eager to boast about his daring escape from prison and how he had tricked the engine driver into giving him a lift in his cab at the front of the train.

"I slept last night in a wood and then walked for miles—" he began.

"Stop!" Ratty cried. "I don't want to hear another word until you have rid yourself of those terrible rags. Go upstairs and change into some of my clothes, quick as you can!"

When Toad came back he was wearing one of Ratty's best suits.

Ratty gave him a good meal, then he said, "Toad, I'm afraid to tell you this, but you can't go back to Toad Hall. It isn't yours any more. The weasels, stoats and ferrets from the Wild Wood have overrun it."

At this news poor Toad burst into tears.

"Pull yourself together, Toad," Ratty urged his friend. "We all thought you would be locked up forever – and many folk said you deserved it too."

"I'll see about all this!" Toad cried, suddenly recovering himself, and he dashed out of Ratty's front door.

On the way to Toad Hall he grabbed a stout stick, but when he approached the front gate a large ferret with a gun fired at him! Toad ducked down, just in time for the bullet to whistle harmlessly over his head. He then scrambled to his feet and scampered back to Ratty's house, now shaking with fury.

Ratty was waiting for him when he
returned. "I won't be beaten!" Toad said
defiantly. "I'll take your boat and approach
Toad Hall by the river. They won't expect
me that way, I'm sure."

But when Toad had rowed only as far as
the bridge, two weasels sent a huge stone
crashing down into the boat, throwing Toad
overboard.

Soaking wet and shivering, Toad made his way back to Ratty's house once more.

As he was drying off by the fire, Mr Badger arrived.

"Welcome home, Toad," he said, solemnly shaking Toad's hand. "It may not be the best homecoming, but I hope that you have learned your lesson. You should be ashamed of yourself for what you did."

Tears began to roll down Toad's cheeks. As he lay sobbing on the sofa, Mole arrived, having heard the news of Toad's return.

"Poor fellow," said Mole. "It must be terrible to lose your home."

"I don't know that there is a lot we can do," said Badger, thoughtfully. "There are stoats on guard all round Toad Hall."

"I agree," said Mole. "We are entirely outnumbered by all those dreadful creatures from the Wild Wood."

"We must think of a plan!" said Ratty.

Toad seemed to finally realise how serious the whole matter was and he burst into tears again.

"Cheer up, Toad," said Badger at last. "There may be a way. I know of an old secret passage that leads into Toad Hall."

"And once we are past the guards," squeaked Mole, grabbing a stick, "we can bop them all on the head and chase the scoundrels out of there!"

Toad was still asleep the next morning
when Ratty came downstairs, but Badger
was already awake, reading the newspaper.

Ratty began gathering swords and pistols.
"What do you think, Mr Badger?" he
asked. "We will have to be well armed if we
are to stand a chance."

"If the plan works," said Badger, "we
will be taking them completely by surprise,
which I'm hoping will mean we should have
no use for anything more than a few good
stout cudgels."

Before Ratty could reply, Mole came in dressed as the old washerwoman. "I went to Toad Hall," he said quietly, "and I told the guards you were planning to launch an attack from the outside!

"I do hope I didn't do the wrong thing," he went on, "but I thought they would believe an old washerwoman."

Both Badger and Ratty could not stop praising Mole's clever idea.

"You acted like a true military general," Badger said. "You will have put them off the scent completely."

"They will mount a guard all round the outside and we will attack from the inside!" cried Ratty.

Only Toad was silent. Mole saw at once that he was growing jealous of all the attention he was being given. So after he had changed back into his own clothes he took Toad outside and asked him to recount his wonderful adventures all over again.

Toad soon forgot his jealousy as Mole listened to his stories.

As soon as it was dark, the four friends gathered in Ratty's parlour. Then, with the air of a conjuror, Ratty produced pistols, swords and cutlasses and handed them to each of the others.

Badger accepted a stout, solid cudgel, but the others were thankful for more fearsome weapons. When everybody agreed they were ready, Badger said he would lead the way.

Badger led them along the path by the river for a short distance, and then dropped over the edge into a dark hole hidden in the bank.

This took everybody by surprise – especially Toad, who slipped and fell into the river with a great *SPLASH*!

Ratty and Mole quickly pulled him out, but Badger was not at all pleased with Toad's clumsiness.

Soon the gallant friends were creeping
along the secret passage into Toad Hall. It
was dark and cold and quite frightening as
their footsteps echoed and the lantern cast
strange shadows on the walls.

Toad was so afraid of being left behind
that he stopped looking where he was
putting his feet. Suddenly he tripped and
bumped into Ratty.

Ratty bumped into Mole and Mole
bumped into Badger, who thought they
were being attacked from the rear, and very
nearly shot at Toad with the pistol Ratty
had finally persuaded him to bring along!

Ratty kept a close eye on Toad after that as they crept along the dark passage. He didn't want Toad to get them into any more trouble.

Presently Badger made a sign and pointed above his head.

"This trap door is the way in," he whispered. "Now, lads, heave away. All together!"

They pushed hard and the heavy trap door creaked open. As they scrambled through they found themselves in the pantry of Toad Hall.

Badger drew himself up to his full height as they heard the sound of shrill laughter coming from the next room.

"Follow me, brave lads!" he ordered.

Then he flung himself against the door to the banqueting hall. At the sight of the battling Badger and his men, the terrified weasels and ferrets tried desperately to escape.

Badger made straight for the Weasel Chief as he sat at the head of a table laden with food. Seeing that the game was up, the Chief took flight and so too did his bodyguards, scrambling and snarling at each other as they knocked over the long table.

Ratty, Toad and Mole all joined the fight until every one of the weasels had fled.

After the battle, Mole went round
collecting all the rifles the weasels and
ferrets had left behind and even asked
Badger if he could keep one for himself.

"Certainly not," said Badger. "But you
have done a fine job, Mole, and the Weasel
Chief has already sent his word that all the
members of his gang will behave themselves
in future and do what we ask."

Mr Toad was so overcome with joy at
being home again that he couldn't speak.

The four friends then sat down to a quiet
supper and wearily headed off to bed.

In the morning Toad announced he was going to give a banquet to celebrate his homecoming. "I'll write out the invitations at once," he said. And he sat down at his desk and busily began writing.

When the invitations were ready one of the weasels even offered to deliver them!

Badger, Ratty and Mole all hoped that Toad would now be cured of his conceited behaviour. But as soon as the invitations had been sent Toad began composing boastful speeches for the banquet.

"Just listen to him," Mole whispered, as they stood outside his door. "He's made up a poem all about himself!"

On the day of the banquet Badger had a very serious talk with Toad. "If you say one boastful word about your foolish deeds," Badger warned, "we will all leave the room and you will be ashamed."

"You're right," said Toad. "I promise I am cured of boasting for ever."

But that night, just before he went to greet his guests, Toad made his boastful speech to the empty chairs in his room – and he felt all the better for it!

With a giggle and a contented sigh, Toad
left his bedroom to join Ratty, Mole and
Badger. They all looked very splendid in
their smart dinner jackets, and Mr Toad felt
very proud of his friends.

All the guests arrived on time, dressed
in their finest clothes. When they saw Toad
standing on the front step of Toad Hall
waiting to greet them, some of them raised
a merry cheer.

Toad did his best to look modest.

"It was nothing, really. Nothing at all," he kept saying over and over again to each guest as he greeted them.

Toad wasn't quite sure himself what he meant, but he was determined to live up to his promise and not disappoint his friends.

After all the excitement had died down and life had returned to normal, Toad and his friends would go for walks together in the Wild Wood.

"There goes famous Mr Toad," Mother Weasel would whisper to her children as they passed by.

She would tell them all about the great
battle in the banqueting hall and about the
fierce Water Rat and the gallant little Mole.
And when her little ones were naughty she
would warn them, "The terrible Mr Badger
will be after you if you don't behave!"

This wasn't really fair to Badger, who
was a gentle fellow at heart and always
fond of small children. But it worked!